For Delilah, Maggie, Spr

– J.D.

First Printing, paperback- published 2014
ISBN: 978-1-312-71345-1
Website: www.maggie-books.com/maggie/
Lulu.com-Maggie Goes Camping

Maggie Goes Camping

Story And Drawings By Julie Davidson

We always go hiking on our camping trips. I love to sing with the birds and meet new friends along the way.

I wonder what I'll find if I follow those birds...

I'm a birdwatching dog!

It's my natural instinct to point out a bird, but these binoculars help.

Look who I found. It's my friend the groundhog.

My friend the groundhog is sometimes called a mouse bear. He looks like a miniature bear when sitting up.

Butterflies can taste with their feet. My paws don't taste very good. "Truman, how do your paws taste?"

Fly fishing takes skill and patience.

"Truman, we have to help him find his family!"

"Truman, we did it! He's safe now with his momma bear."

"Truman, I love to watch the sunset with you."

It's so beautiful to stargaze at night. I wish upon a star that I will always be able to spend time camping with my friends.

There wasn't anything scary in the woods. It was just all the friends we made along the way.

Look who I found. It's my friend the groundhog.

My friend the groundhog is sometimes called a mouse bear. He looks like a miniature bear when sitting up.